Dear Parents:

Congratulations! Your child is taking the first steps on an exciting journey. The destination? Independent reading!

STEP INTO READING® will help your child get there. The program offers five steps to reading success. Each step includes fun stories and colorful art or photographs. In addition to original fiction and books with favorite characters, there are Step into Reading Non-Fiction Readers, Phonics Readers and Boxed Sets, Sticker Readers, and Comic Readers—a complete literacy program with something to interest every child.

Learning to Read, Step by Step!

Ready to Read   Preschool–Kindergarten
• big type and easy words • rhyme and rhythm • picture clues
For children who know the alphabet and are eager to begin reading.

Reading with Help   Preschool–Grade 1
• basic vocabulary • short sentences • simple stories
For children who recognize familiar words and sound out new words with help.

Reading on Your Own   Grades 1–3
• engaging characters • easy-to-follow plots • popular topics
For children who are ready to read on their own.

Reading Paragraphs   Grades 2–3
• challenging vocabulary • short paragraphs • exciting stories
For newly independent readers who read simple sentences with confidence.

Ready for Chapters   Grades 2–4
• chapters • longer paragraphs • full-color art
For children who want to take the plunge into chapter books but still like colorful pictures.

STEP INTO READING® is designed to give every child a successful reading experience. The grade levels are only guides; children will progress through the steps at their own speed, developing confidence in their reading. The F&P Text Level on the back cover serves as another tool to help you choose the right book for your child.

Remember, a lifetime love of reading starts with a single step!

For Latoya

PJJ
GREEN

Text copyright © 2021 by Suzanne Lang
Cover art and interior illustrations copyright © 2021 by Max Lang

Step into Reading, Random House, and the Random House colophon are registered trademarks
of Penguin Random House LLC.

GRUMPY MONKEY is a registered trademark of Pick & Flick Pictures, Inc.

Visit us on the Web!
StepIntoReading.com
rhcbooks.com

Educators and librarians, for a variety of teaching tools,
visit us at RHTeachersLibrarians.com

Library of Congress Cataloging-in-Publication Data is available upon request.
ISBN 978-0-593-42831-3 (trade) — ISBN 978-0-593-42835-1 (lib. bdg.) —
ISBN 978-0-593-42862-7 (ebook)

Printed in the United States of America
10 9 8 7 6 5 4 3 2 1

This book has been officially leveled by using
the F&P Text Level Gradient™ Leveling System.

GRUMPY MONKEY
Ready, Set, Bananas!

by Suzanne Lang
illustrated by Max Lang

Random House 🏠 New York

It was the day of
the big race.
Jim was excited.
He loved Race Day.

The animals headed to
the starting line
to watch the race.

Now it was quiet
on Jim's side
of the jungle.
That made him happy.

Jim settled in
for a nap.

He had a dream.

It was raining bananas.

"Ouch!"

Jim woke up.
Tortoise was tapping
Jim on the head.
"Jim! Jim!
Are you awake?"
she asked.

"I am now,"
said Jim.
He was one
grumpy monkey.

"I want to race,"
said Tortoise.
"You are in
the wrong place,"
said Jim.

"I can run faster
if you carry me,"
said Tortoise.

"No!"

said Jim.

"Please?"

Jim and Tortoise got
to the starting line
just in time.

Water Buffalo
called out,
"Ready. Set . . ."

"Go!"

squawked Oxpecker.

"Go! Go! Go! Go! Go!

I LOVE RACE DAY!"

Leslie was in the lead,
with Marabou
right behind her.

Then Porcupine came
out of nowhere
and ran past them!

"Faster! Faster!"

shouted Tortoise.

Norman swung
next to the racers.
"Go, Jim, go!"
he cheered.

Jim and Tortoise
ran faster.

Norman swung into
the banana tree.

"It's raining bananas!"
shouted Porcupine.

"No, Jim!
Do not stop!
Keep running!"
said Tortoise.
But Jim wanted
a banana.

"Look at all the bananas!" shouted the animals. "Hooray!"

Tortoise stayed

in the race.

She crossed the
finish line.
"I won! I won!"
Tortoise shouted.

"This is a dream come true," said Jim.

Norman agreed.

It was another great
Race Day.